Alice's Musical Debut

by DuEwa Frazier

Illustrated by Nadia Salas

Alice's Musical Debut

by DuEwa Frazier

Illustrated by Nadia Salas

Other books by DuEwa Frazier

Quincy Rules (2016)

Deanne in the Middle (2014)

Goddess Under the Bridge: Poems (2013)

Ten Marbles and a Bag to Put Them In: Poems for Children (2010)

Check the Rhyme: An Anthology of Female Poets & Emcees (2006)

Shedding Light From My Journeys (2002)

Alice's Musical Debut

by DuEwa Frazier

Illustrated by Nadia Salas

Lit Noire Publishing children.™

www.litnoirepublishing.co
www.duewaworld.com

Library of Congress Control Number: 2019902708

Alice's musical debut/ DuEwa Frazier.

ISBN-13:978-1539945550(paperback)

Disclaimer: This story is a work of historical fiction.

For Alice Coltrane and Virginia Hamilton

Alice's Musical Debut

Somewhere in the heart of Detroit,
Alice McLeod cannot sleep.

She hears the *pop* and *rumble*
of a storm.

Alice's room shakes from the *BOOM* of
even louder thunder. And then she hears
the *crackle* and *snap* of lightning. Alice
hears tree branches break and fall to
the ground. She rushes out of bed to
look out through her window.

3

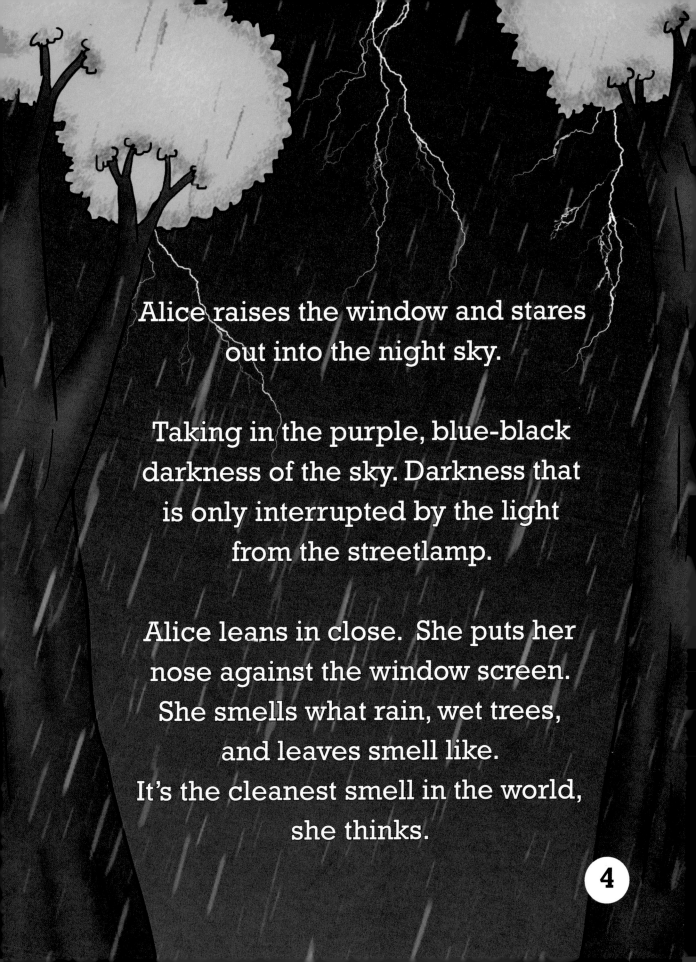

Alice raises the window and stares
out into the night sky.

Taking in the purple, blue-black
darkness of the sky. Darkness that
is only interrupted by the light
from the streetlamp.

Alice leans in close. She puts her
nose against the window screen.
She smells what rain, wet trees,
and leaves smell like.
It's the cleanest smell in the world,
she thinks.

Alice closes her eyes and listens. *Plunk.*

Alice come closer." *Plunk.*

"Alice come closer." *Plunk. Plunk. Plunk.*

The raindrops talk to her.

Did the rain just say, *'Alice come closer'?*

Surely it didn't.

Alice hears the rustle of the leaves in the trees. *Swish.*

"Alice come closer."

Swish. *"Alice come closer."* *Swish. Swish. Swish.*

The leaves talk to her.

Did the leaves just say, *'Alice come closer'?*

Alice hears an owl that is perched high
up in the tree, near her bedroom window.
"Hoot. Alice come closer. Hoot.
Alice come closer. Hoot. Hoot. Hoot.
Who is the little owl talking to?

The owl is talking.

So are the trees
and the rain.

All of their sounds
together are like
musical instruments,
in an accidental band,
beckoning Alice to
make her own sounds
with nature.

And so Alice begins to hum.

While the thunder *rumbles*

and the lightning *claps*,

while the rain *plunks*,

and the trees *swish*,

while the owl *hoots*,

Alice falls asleep.

8

9

The next day, Alice steps outside after breakfast.

The warm sun greets her as she sits on the front porch.

Alice looks up at the sky, admiring the formation of faint clouds dancing around the sunlight.

One cloud looks like a smiling cat's face.

Another looks like a train car.

A third cloud looks like a balloon.

Alice sees a formation of birds flying in the sky. She wonders where they're going.

Alice picks a few dandelions from the grass near the front steps. She blows the dandelions and their seeds sail off into the air, to find a new home. *Whish. Whish. Whish.*

Here come the bees. Alice feels their vibration and begins to mimic their sound.

Bzzzzzzz.

Bzzzzzzzz.

Alice talks to the bees

"Bees don't you sting me because I want to play.
I'm going to jump rope, play hop scotch
and patty cake today."

It's as if the bees took note
of Alice's command.
They *buzzed* away to some
nearby flowers.

Later that day,
Alice's friend
Shelly comes by.
Shelly runs up
to hug Alice.

"Alice let's play patty cake."
The girls clap their hands.

15

"Patty cake, patty cake... Baker's man...
Put it in the oven as fast as you can."

After Alice and Shelly play patty cake
and jump rope, Alice says, "Let's sing songs.
I have one I can teach you."

Alice sings to Shelly and teaches her the song.
Listen to the ringing of the leaves
as the trees sway with the breeze.
Listen to the whistle and chirp
of the birds sitting high in the trees.
Listen to the whirring
of the pinwheels in the front yard.
Listen to the sound of the airplanes whizzing
in the sky.
We can make music with our hands.
Clap. Clap. Clap.
We can make music with our feet.
Stomp. Stomp. Stomp.
We can make music with our fingers.
Snap. Snap. Snap.

16

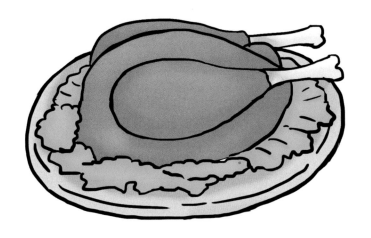

Alice and Shelly work up a good appetite.

Shelly eats a delicious lunch with Alice.
Mrs. McLeod fixes sweet iced tea, potato salad,
turkey sandwiches, and cookies for desert.

After Shelly goes home, Alice's mother has a
surprise for her.

"Alice, I hear you humming and singing all of the time. I think it's time I start you on piano lessons."

Alice feels her knees become weak.
Her stomach feels loose and jiggly like jelly.

"Piano lessons mama? I don't want to play piano."

Alice's mother looks disappointed.

"Baby, your father and I think you have such an ear for musical rhythms. Piano would be good for you Alice."

Alice turns away and runs. Her mother calls after her.

"Alice...Alice..."

19

Alice runs out the door to the backyard.

Feeling overwhelmed by her mother's request to play piano, Alice sits in the grass among everything that is alive.

Alice loves all sound that makes music on its own. Nature is where she feels free.

Alice watches the blades of grass twitch with the climbing of ladybugs. Alice doesn't mind the ladybugs crawling on her face or the bees *buzzing* above her head.

Alice closes her eyes and listens. She hears the struggling sound of a car engine that won't start next door. She hears the laughter of children jumping rope down the street. She hears the tinkle of the bell in the ice cream man's truck.

Suddenly, Alice hears a magnificent sound that comes to grab her. She hears the sound of the piano coming from her house. Her mother plays and sings, "Amazing Grace."

Alice has never heard her mother sing like this. She opens her eyes and wants to see what her mother looks like. Alice wants to feel the vibration of the piano up close.

There in the family room, Alice sees her mother. Mrs. McLeod's head is thrown back. Her eyes closed tightly, she sings from her heart.

27

Still singing, Alice's mother takes her hand, guiding her to play the piano. Alice sways and hums with the music. After some time, Alice's mother stops singing and playing.

Now it is only Alice playing the piano. Closing her eyes, Alice plays the piano as if she has done it a hundred times. She feels the rhythm and vibration of love all around her.

Alice becomes the music.

The End

About Alice Coltrane (Alice McLeod)

Alice Coltrane was a celebrated jazz pianist, harpist, composer and organist. She was born Alice McLeod on August 27, 1937 in "Motor City" Detroit, Michigan. She grew up in Mt. Olive Baptist Church. Learning church hymnals gave Alice a foundation in spiritual music. Her parents, Solon and Ann McLeod loved music. Alice's mother Ann played piano and was known for her beautiful alto voice. Her parent's love for music spread to Alice.

Alice learned to play piano at the age of seven and studied the classical musical styles of great composers. It was at Mt. Olive Baptist Church that Alice learned to play piano and organ for the church's choirs: the Senior Choir, the Pastor's Choir, and the Young People's Choir. Alice also trained at the Mack Avenue Church of God in Christ with the Lemon Gospel Choir. Mack Avenue was also the musical home for Deloris Hanson and David Winans, parents of Detroit's most famous gospel singing family – the Winans!

Alice McLeod went on to master the organ and harp in addition to playing the piano. Alice became a sought-after musician in Detroit, Michigan. Alice married the late, great, avant-garde jazz musician John Coltrane in 1965. She and John had four children: Michele, John Jr., Oranyan, and Ravi. She became Alice Coltrane and together with her husband, created several jazz recordings including *Cosmic Music, Live in Japan*, and *Expressions*. One of their best-known collaborations is titled *Love Supreme*, a favorite among jazz lovers. Alice Coltrane recorded more than twenty albums over a thirty-year span including: *The Impulse Story* (2006), *Translinear Light* (2004; with Ravi Coltrane), and *The Music of Alice Coltrane: Astral Meditations* (1999). Alice Coltrane passed away on January 12, 2007 at the age of 69.

Reader Questions

1. What are three things you like about this story?

2. List the sounds from nature that Alice hears.

3. Describe Alice's mother.

4. What makes Shelly a good friend to Alice?

5. Why do you think Alice was reluctant to play the piano at first?

Made in the USA
Monee, IL
11 November 2019